Jack and the Zonkalins

Jack and the Zonkalins

Jenny Crossley

Dedicated to Brian and Margaret

Jack ran into the garden behind his house.

He spotted a rainbow in the sky.

"Wow," said Jack.

He had seen rainbows before, but this one was special.

It landed right at the end of his garden.

Jack ran to the rainbow.
He had heard that leprechauns and their pot of gold could be found there.
What would Jack find?

When Jack reached the rainbow, his wish came true.
A friendly leprechaun, dressed from head to toe in green was there.
But there was no pot of gold.

"Hello, Mr. Leprechaun," said Jack.
"Where's your pot of gold?"
The leprechaun looked glum.
"The zonkalins stole it," he said.
"Now those naughty zonkalins are having a competition to ge
rid of the rainbow."

The leprechaun was right.

The colour violet had disappeared from the rainbow.

There were only six colours left.

Red, orange, yellow, green, blue and indigo.

The rainbow looked very strange indeed.

"What will happen if the whole rainbow disappears?" asked Jack.
"It will rain all day, every day for seven days," said the leprechaun.
"We must try to stop them and get my pot of gold back. Will you help me?"
"How long will it take?" asked Jack.
"Only a few seconds of human time," said the leprechaun.
"When you're with me, time stands still. Take my hand. We're going to run around the end of the rainbow three times and then jump into it."

Jack took the leprechaun's hand.

"One, two, three, go!" said the leprechaun.

After running around it three times, Jack felt very dizzy.

"Jump now," said the leprechaun.

They both jumped into the end of the rainbow.

Whoosh!
Jack felt himself falling right down into a black hole.
He felt very scared. He wondered if he would hurt himself when he landed.

Suddenly, he landed on something soft.
He hoped it wasn't the leprechaun.
Luckily, he was sitting on a pile of straw.
Phew, what a relief!

"Listen," said the leprechaun.
"I can hear noises coming from over there. Let's go and see what's happening."
They went around a corner and were amazed by what they saw.

"I was right!" said the leprechaun. "It's the zonkalins!
Jack was amazed by what he saw!
Zonkalins were goblins with wonky noses.
Some zonkalins had long, pointed noses.
Other zonkalins had spiral noses, or noses that pointed to one side.

The zonkalins were taking coins out of the pot of gold.
Above them was the rainbow's end.
Jack could see the different colours.

The zonkalins threw the gold coins at each colour.
One of the zonkalins hit the indigo colour and it disappeared.
All the zonkalins cheered with delight.
"Bring on the rain, ha ha ha," shouted one zonkalin.

"This is terrible," said the leprechaun.
"When all the colours are gone, the rainbow will disappear and it will start to rain.
Then the zonkalins will gather up my gold coins and run away. We have to stop them."
"I'm a bit scared of them," said Jack.
"Just take a deep breath and stay calm," said the leprechaun.
"If you take their attention away from the rainbow, I'll gather up the coins."

"You're on!" said Jack.
"I'll do cartwheels and handstands. That should get their attention!"
"Good idea!" said the leprechaun.

Jack ran over to the other side of the cave.
"Look at me!" he shouted at the zonkalins.
They stopped throwing coins and looked at him in amazement.
They had never seen a little boy before.

Jack did two cartwheels.

The zonkalins gasped in amazement and dropped the coins.

Jack did a handstand and walked on his hands.

The zonkalins started to follow him.

The leprechaun took his chance and ran to the pot of gold.
He gathered the coins and put them into the pot.
At the other side of the cave, Jack kept the zonkalins busy.
He showed them how to do cartwheels.

The zonkalins were very dizzy now and sat on the ground.
Quick Jack," called the leprechaun. "Let's go now!"
Jack and the leprechaun made their escape with the pot of gold.

They ran to the entrance to the cave.

"Oh, no!" said Jack. "How do we get back up? We fell down, but we can't fall back up! It's just not possible!"

"It's a bit more difficult getting back up," said the leprechaun.

"I have to sing the leprechaun song from start to finish. Then we'll be able to fly to the top."

"Hurry up and sing it," said Jack. "Here come the zonkalins!"

The leprechaun started singing:
"I'm a little leprechaun, all dressed in green,
Friendly and helpful, I'm very seldom seen.
If you do see me, let the truth be told,
I'm at the rainbow's end with a great big pot of gold."

At the end of the song, he took Jack's hand and they started to fly.
"Help", cried Jack. "There's a zonkalin hanging onto my leg!"
"Tickle his hand," said the leprechaun. "They hate being tickled."
Jack leant over and tickled the zonkalin's hand.
The zonkalin let go of his grip and fell onto the straw.

Jack and the leprechaun were back in Jack's garden again.
All the colours of the rainbow had returned.
Red, orange, yellow, green, blue, indigo and violet.
The rainbow looked beautiful.

"Thank you for your help, Jack," said the leprechaun.
Then he disappeared along with his pot of gold.
Jack looked proudly at the rainbow.
He had helped to bring it back again and would never forget his exciting day with the leprechaun.

Made in the USA
Monee, IL
20 January 2023

24577267R00019